TOM & TALLULAH
AND THE
WITCHES' FEAST

Books by Vivian French

The Adventures of Alfie Onion

The Cherry Pie Princess

Tom & Tallulah and the Witches' Feast

TOM & TALLULAH
AND THE
WITCHES' FEAST

VIVIAN FRENCH
illustrated by Marta Kissi

Kane Miller
A DIVISION OF EDC PUBLISHING

First American Edition 2018
Kane Miller, A Division of EDC Publishing

Text © 2018 Vivian French
Illustrations © 2018 Marta Dlugolecka
Published by arrangement with Walker Books Limited, London.

For information contact:
Kane Miller, A Division of EDC Publishing
P.O. Box 470663
Tulsa, OK 74147-0663
www.kanemiller.com
www.edcpub.com
www.usbornebooksandmore.com

Library of Congress Control Number: 2017942427

Printed and bound in the United States of America
1 2 3 4 5 6 7 8 9 10
ISBN: 978-1-61067-734-9

For Letitia May, with love
from Ralph, Bertie and Leilah

For James, with all my love, always
M.K.

Chapter One

"Toast the toad and baste the bat,
Mash the mouse tails, roast the rat,
Steam the snails and slice the slugs,
Don't forget to boil the bugs.
Prick a pimple with a pin,
Let our meeting now begin!"

As the final words died away, the witches of the Chumley Charmed Circle turned towards their leader. Madam Mavis Mortlock stepped forward, bowing graciously to the left and right.

"Welcome, sister witches! May your broomsticks fly high among the stars, your toads be super warty, and your spells be ever—" The head witch stopped. "Aren't we missing someone?"

"I think we're all here, dear." A comfortably rounded witch was counting on her fingers. "Three, four, five. Or did I forget me?" She counted again. "Yes. Five of us. Isn't that right? Or are we expecting darling Tabitha Tickle?"

An elderly witch with cold beady eyes snorted loudly. "Of course we aren't, Dolly. She's mad as a box of frogs. She hasn't been to a meeting for months!"

Madam Mavis tutted disapprovingly. "Really, Gertrude! That's no way to speak of a much-loved friend and colleague.

And, Dolly – we're waiting for her granddaughter, our little apprentice."

"Tallulah Tickle is late. Again." Gertrude's voice was as cold as her eyes. "I said from the start it was ridiculous to ask her to join us. We should have chosen someone of mature years. I have an excellent suggestion—"

Before Madam Mavis could answer there was a loud *whoosh!* and a very young witch crash-landed her broomstick in the middle of the circle.

The witches jumped backward, and Leonora Danglefin sat down with an undignified thump. Madam Mavis, taken by surprise, staggered sideways and clutched at her companions – and they all collapsed into an exceptionally prickly gorse bush.

"Sorry, sorry, sorry, sorry!" Tallulah was pink with embarrassment. "I'm so, so, so sorry – I thought I'd left loads of time." She picked up her broomstick and scurried to the edge of the circle, her little cat at her heels. "But it's OK, I'm here now..."

"It is not OK!" The head witch heaved herself out of the gorse bush, rubbing the painful scratches on her arms. "Our Charmed Circle is a serious and exclusive group, Tallulah Tickle."

There was a murmur of agreement, and a shrill cry of, "Hear, hear!"

"Thank you, Gertrude." Madam Mavis gave her a brief nod. "Tallulah, you have talent, or I would never have invited you to join us—" the head witch chose to ignore Gertrude's contemptuous sniff— "but I think I might have made a mistake. You've been late for every meeting, your broomstick control is deplorably unreliable, and your cakes are burnt to a cinder. And now this wild arrival, upsetting all our members. Tallulah, I'm afraid you can no longer be the Chumley Charmed Circle's apprentice witch."

"But Madam Mavis, I brought a cake!" Tallulah's eyes were brimming with tears as she pulled a battered cardboard box out of her bag. "And I tried really hard with it. I know the last one was burnt, but this one's much better – it's hardly burnt at all—"

"That's enough!" Madam Mavis shook her head. "I don't want to hear any more."

As Tallulah put the box back in her bag and picked up her broomstick, sniffing as she did so, Gertrude Higgins sidled over to the head witch.

"A word in your ear, Mavis. Might I mention my good friend Enid Teazle? She'd be only too pleased to join our happy band."

Madam Mavis found Gertrude irritating at the best of times, and Tallulah's tears were softening her elderly heart. Thinking fast, she shook her head.

"Not now, Gertrude. You know the rules! When a witch is expelled from a charmed circle, she is given one last chance to redeem herself."

Tallulah looked up hopefully, but Gertrude Higgins raised her eyebrows. "Is that so, Madam Mavis? I've never heard of any such rule. So, do tell us! What happens next?"

Tallulah, hardly daring to breathe, clutched her bag to her chest while she waited for Madam Mavis to speak. The head witch was looking thoughtful as she walked towards the center of the circle.

"We will set Tallulah a task," she announced,

"and if she succeeds, she
will regain her place."

Gertrude Higgins
brightened. She knew
Tallulah's weakness,
and she leaned forward
eagerly. "Might I suggest
Tallulah cooks us all
a Midnight Feast?"

"Oh YES!" Leonora Danglefin was enthusiastic.
"You're so clever, Gertrude!"

Dulcie, who always agreed with Leonora,
nodded. "So clever!"

Even Miss Dolly joined in the applause. Feasts
were very popular among the witches, especially
if cooked by someone else.

Madam Mavis, who had intended to suggest
something simpler, was forced to agree. "It's
decided. You will provide a Midnight Feast,
Tallulah. Shall we say at the next full moon?"

Gertrude's eyes gleamed. "No, no! We mustn't keep her waiting … it's my birthday on Friday. Let's have our feast then."

"This Friday?" Madam Mavis was horrified. "But that's only three days away!"

"Too much for little Tallulah?" Gertrude enquired with a sneer.

Tallulah was very pale. "Friday? I can do that."

"A Midnight Feast on Friday." Leonora and Dulcie beamed. "How wonderful!"

"And – oh my word! I've had another idea." Gertrude snapped her fingers. "Why don't we each think of our favorite food? So Tallulah can cook it for us!"

Tallulah swallowed bravely. "I'll do my best. What's your favorite, Madam Mavis?"

"Macaroni and cheese," the head witch said firmly.

"And you, Miss Higgins?"

"Aha!" Gertrude's smile was triumphant, and

Mavis looked at her in alarm. "Let's make it into a little game! We'll each write the name of our favorite food on a piece of paper, but we won't look to see what anyone else has written. And I'll keep the papers safe. If Tallulah Tickle has a genuine talent for magic she'll have no trouble guessing what we've chosen."

Mavis looked at Tallulah. "Does that sound fair to you, Tallulah?"

She was certain Tallulah would say the task was impossible, but the girl nodded.

"I'll be here on Friday," she said. And after a curtsy to Madam Mavis, she climbed onto her broomstick. Her skinny little cat hopped on behind her, and the two of them flew away.

Gertrude Higgins looked after her with a satisfied smile. "I think it's fair to say we won't be seeing HER again."

"I think she's very brave," said Madam Mavis. "That's a remarkably difficult task you've set, but she's determined to have a try. And I'll look after the papers, Gertrude, if you don't mind." She held out her hand, and a small metal box appeared. "We'll keep them in here."

It was obvious that Gertrude *did* mind, but she did her best to smile. "Of course, Mavis dear. Whatever you say." She pulled a scrap of paper from her pocket and scribbled on it at some length before folding it neatly and dropping it into the box.

The head witch suppressed a sigh. *That'll be something complicated*, she thought. *What a shame. I can't see how Tallulah can possibly win.*

Chapter Two

TOM TICKLE sniffed the air and frowned. "Tallulah's burned something," he said to himself as he walked up the path towards the tiny cottage crouched between two tall trees. "Oh dear. She'll be cross. Let's hope we get some supper."

Reaching the cottage, he stopped in surprise. "That's odd," he said. "The door's open…" He stepped inside and called, "Tallulah?"

The only answer was a swirl of black smoke and a crash from the kitchen. Tom hurried to see what was going on, and found his sister surrounded by burnt saucepans, cookbooks and a jar of flour. Sparks, the little black cat, was sitting on the end of the table looking worried.

"*Meow*," she said. "Things aren't good."

Tom's eyes widened. "I can see that… Lou! Whatever are you doing?"

"Cooking." Tallulah picked up a wooden spoon and began stirring a murky yellow substance in one of the pans. "I'm trying to make macaroni and cheese."

"Macaroni and cheese?" Tom stared. "But you can't cook."

Tallulah flung down the spoon and burst into floods of tears. "I know!" she wailed. "But if I don't learn how to make macaroni and cheese by Friday I'll be thrown out of the Charmed Circle because that horrible Gertrude Higgins absolutely hates me and I want to be a witch more than anything else in the whole wide world!"

"Lou … you're going to have to explain." Tom sat down at the table.

Tallulah sank down beside him and, with much nose blowing and sniffing, began to describe the events of the evening. It took Tom

some time to unravel the details, but at last he understood what had happened.

"What on earth made you say you'd do such a thing?" he demanded. "Nobody could possibly guess five different favorite foods, let alone cook them!"

A determined expression crossed his sister's face. "I want to be a real witch, Tom. I have to make them take me back. If I do well, they'll make me a full member of the Charmed Circle … and then I'll be able to make Grandmother better." She blew her nose hard.

Tom's eyebrows rose. "Lou! You're mad! Almost as mad as Grandmother, and that's about as mad as you can get."

"No, I'm not." Tallulah put her hand on his arm. "Grandmother's a witch, right?"

Tom hesitated. "Well … she was until she started thinking she was a bird of some kind."

Sparks nodded. "*Meow*. A chicken."

"Whereas Mother and Father were just ordinary," Tallulah said. "If Father had been even the least little bit good at magic he'd have noticed the barn roof was about to fall in on him and Mother … but he didn't. And that made us orphans. You were only a baby, so you won't remember. But we never had to worry, because we had our darling witchy grandmother."

Tom looked doubtful. "She may have been a witch, but she didn't do any magic when she was looking after us."

"Yes, she did," Tallulah said. "Don't you remember her cooking? She just put on her hat, tapped the plates, and – ZING! PING! Delicious dinners." She sighed. "I wish I could do that."

"Me too," Tom agreed, with rather too much enthusiasm. "I loved her dinners."

Tallulah's face changed. "And you don't like mine?"

"Oh yes – I do." Tom did his best to sound enthusiastic.

"Grandmother looked after us, so now it's up to me to look after her," Tallulah said. "And supposing she really did change into something horrible? Oh, Tom! What would we do then?"

Tom took his spectacles off and wiped them. It was unusual for his sister to ask his advice on anything and he was taken by surprise. It was nearly six months since he and Tallulah had woken one morning to find their grandmother missing. She had been to a meeting of the Charmed Circle the night before, but the children had been asleep when she got back. Two dirty cups and plates suggested she had come home with someone else, but there was no clue as to who it was. Sparks, Tabitha's usual companion, had seen nothing; she had spent the evening curled up on Tallulah's pillow.

After an anxious search the children had discovered their grandmother in the garden shed, together with her bed, her alarm clock

and a bunch of flowers. She was muttering to herself, and when they asked if she was all right she peered at them as if she had never seen them before. *"La-di-da-di-doo-da! Beware, children, beware!"* And then she had shaken her head as if to clear it. "My dears … forgive me. I'm not well … not well at all. *Oh la la la! Here I go again… Squawk! Squawk! Doo-diddle-dee!"*

Since then she had refused to leave the shed, and Tallulah and Tom had had to manage as best they could. At first there were one or two

moments every day when they could ask questions
– such as, "Where do clean socks come from?" –
and get reasonably helpful answers, but eventually
these moments vanished altogether. Grandmother's
appearance remained much the same, but she
became increasingly good at perching on the
end of her bed and had a tendency to believe her
infrequent visitors were foxes who must not be
allowed anywhere near her.

Tom was aware that his sister's life had not
been easy. As well as taking her grandmother's
place in the Chumley Charmed Circle, Tallulah
had taken over running the household. She did
all the washing, the cooking and the cleaning. She
didn't do it very well, and she was often cross and
grumpy, but she tried her best.

He stood up and gave her a hug. "I'll help you,
Lou," he said. "If that's what you want."

"It's exactly what I want." Tallulah was
emphatic. "I really miss her."

"And me," Tom said. "I miss her lots!"

Tallulah shook her head as she pushed him away. "It's different for me, Tom. I'm here to look after you, but there's no one to look after me."

"Oh." This had never occurred to Tom. "I can look after you, Lou! At least … I can try."

Tallulah gave a dismissive snort. "Thanks – but you're my little brother. No. I've decided. I'm going to join the Charmed Circle, and make sure Grandmother gets better. Then things will be just like they used to be."

"OK," Tom said. "Let's make a plan."

"Hurrah!" Tallulah cheered up immediately. "I know just what you need to do!"

"Me?" Tom blinked.

"Yes! None of the witches have ever met you. We never talk about families, just like I never tell you about the Charmed Circle, so they won't know who you are. So you can be the one who finds out their favorite meals!"

Tom looked alarmed. "I don't—" he began, but his sister gave him a stern look.

"You can't change your mind, Tom. You said you'd help. All you have to do is go and ask them. Well – you might have to be a bit cunning about it. But I'll help you think of something!"

"Oh…" Tom swallowed. "That is … OK. I mean: yes."

Chapter Three

"'THANK YOOOOOOU, Gertrude!'" Gertrude Higgins sneered, and spat into the bushes. "'Not now, Gertrude!' 'Tiddlyumpty toodleoo, Gertrude!' *Grrrr* ... who does she think she is? Madam Snooty Pooty Know-It-All Mavis, that's who. But my time will come – and then she'll sing a different song. It'll be, 'Yes, Ms. Higgins!' and, 'Of course, Ms. Higgins! Whatever you say, Ms. Higgins!'"

Gertrude was stamping along the path that led to her cramped room at the bottom of an ivy-covered tower, muttering as she went.

After Tallulah's departure from the Charmed Circle, Madam Mavis had delivered a lecture on Kindness and Consideration for Others, followed by a list of requests from the local villagers for help with spasms, goiters, curious lumps and misbehaving chickens. Each of these had been dealt with in turn, but every successful spell had made Gertrude more and more angry. "Kindness? Consideration for others? Making people better? What kind of pathetic witchcraft is that?!"

Gertrude had hidden her feelings at the time, but as she left she had kicked her broomstick so hard it had turned sulky and insisted on landing two miles from home. Now she was dragging it along, muttering to herself. Her cat, Kibble, pattered behind her. He was wondering if there would be any supper. Gertrude was not generous with food – or, indeed, anything else.

"Rrrk! Rrrk!" A large toad came hopping out from under a bush, and Gertrude peered at it.

"Ha! Has anyone been snooping?"

The toad spat. "Want my supper."

"You'll get your supper. Now – has anyone been here?"

"Nah." The toad shook its head. "Want supper now."

"Kibble! Get the toad his worms." As the cat went to collect the jar of worms, Gertrude unlocked the heavy wooden door that led to her cluttered room.

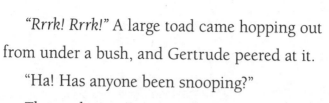

Once inside she made herself a cheese sandwich, cutting the cheese so thin that it was almost transparent. Seeing Kibble's hopeful expression, she pointed to the kipper bones lying on the floor. "Plenty left on those, Kibble. And remember! As soon as I'm leader of the Chumley Charmed Circle we'll be living a very different life."

"Can't come soon enough," Kibble muttered. "I'm starving."

Gertrude ignored him and sat down at her table. Moving a vase of roses out of the way, she pulled a large black book towards her and opened it at a well-thumbed page.

"Let me see, let me see… 'Once the spell is cast, refresh regularly on a monthly basis.'" As she peered more closely at the words, she pushed her crusts to the side of her plate. At once Kibble jumped onto the table, purring loudly.

"No, Kibble! Waste not, want not! I'll save those

for tomorrow. Go and eat your kipper bones."
Gertrude gave the cat a push and he fell off the
table with a yowl.

After a furtive glance over her shoulder, the
witch bent over the book once more. Black
Magic was strictly forbidden by Madam Mavis,
but Gertrude had other ideas. She had moved
to Chumley after a band of angry farmers in her
previous village had set fire to her house; they
had not appreciated two-headed cows or purple
flying pigs. After writing herself several glowing
references she had been invited to join the
Chumley Charmed Circle,
and she was now working
on her plan to
take it over.

"I haven't gotten rid of Tabitha Tickle yet, but it won't be long." Gertrude gave a self-satisfied chuckle. "And I've made sure her nasty little granddaughter will fail miserably." She chuckled again. "Watch out, Madam Mavis! Goody-goody little Miss Dolly's on her side, but Leonora and Dulcie will do as I say ... so once those Tickles have gone, I'll call for a vote – and it'll be three against two. And then who'll be head witch? Me, me, ME! There'll be no more Kindness and Consideration for Others ... oh, no. It'll be warts and whiskers for anyone who crosses me. Heh, heh, heh!" Gertrude Higgins cackled so loudly that Kibble put his paws over his ears. "I'll be ordering peaches and cream and puddings and pies from the Chumley villagers ... yes, pies, Kibble! And all for free. No more scrimping and saving, no more counting every penny. A sheep that moos, a cow that barks, a hen that lays bad eggs – a couple of spells like that and I'll have every man, woman and child fighting to bring me the best they have."

Kibble, encouraged by the mention of pies, jumped back onto the table. Gertrude was concentrating too hard to notice.

She was checking the final instructions of one of the wickedest spells of all: a spell to turn witches into chickens.

Chapter Four

TALLULAH'S SUPPER was not a success. The
macaroni and cheese was solid and tasted of soot.
Tom gave up after a couple of mouthfuls and
made himself a jam sandwich, but Tallulah
struggled on.

"Yum," she said as she put her knife and fork
down on her empty plate. "Delicious. Well …
maybe not exactly delicious. But at least I could
eat it. Take some to Grandmother, Tom." She
carved a slab. "Here you are."

Taking the plate, Tom set off for Grandmother's
shed. Opening the door he heard muttering and

as he stepped inside a mouse
came hurtling out, followed
by a loud squawk.

"Hi, Grandmother! I've
brought your supper. It's
macaroni…" Tom stopped.
He was used to seeing his
grandmother on the end of
the bed, but now she was perched on a shelf.
"Grandmother! What are you doing?"

Tabitha Tickle peered at him over her little
gold spectacles. "Whiskery weasels! A visitor! Do I
know you, young man?"

"It's me, Grandmother: Tom. Your
grandson, remember?"

Tabitha blinked. "Tom…" She
rubbed at her ear, and Tom
noticed with alarm
that the back of

her hand was covered in scales.

Oh no, he thought. *What's happening to her? They almost look like chicken scales…* He pushed the thought away and smiled at his grandmother, who was still looking confused.

"Let me see, let me see. *La-la-fiddle-di-dee.* Tom … Tom … Tom. Aha!" Her eyes brightened. "You're Timothy's boy!"

Tom nodded. "That's right. And I've brought you your supper."

Tabitha sat up on her shelf and sniffed. "What is it? Smells of soot."

"It did get a bit burned," Tom agreed. "It's macaroni and cheese. Tallulah made it."

His grandmother sniffed again. "And who might she be? A bibbity bobbity bunny?"

Tom passed up the plate, and his grandmother seized the congealed lump of pasta in both hands. She took a large bite, then coughed and spat it out.

"Disgusting," she announced. "Fetch me a

worm. And tell the cook to talk to… help me out, boy, you know who I mean. A witch that cooks. Makes the best macaroni and cheese in the county…"

Tom scratched his head. There was only one name he could remember. "Gertrude Higgins?"

"ARRRRRRRRRRRRRRRRGH!" He jumped as his grandmother let out a terrifying roar and glared at him, trembling with rage. "HIDEOUS boy!"

"I'm very sorry, Grandmother." Tom backed hastily away. "I didn't mean to upset you … that's the only name I know."

Tabitha's expression softened a little. "Humph! That woman's a tiddly widdly piddly toad. Never liked her, never will … never never never … *la la*

… *diddly doo*…" Her voice faded, and Tom saw her eyes were closing.

"Grandmother?" he said, but there was no answer. Picking up the plate, he made his way back to the cottage.

"Well?" Tallulah asked. "Did she like it?"

Tom shook his head. "No. And I'll tell you something scary, Lou. I'm sure I saw scales on her hands. You don't think she's really going to turn into some kind of bird, do you?"

Tallulah sighed. "Actually, Tom, I do."

"So how do we stop it happening?" Tom asked.

"Don't you ever listen?" Tallulah sounded weary. "I *told* you. I have to be a proper witch, not just an apprentice. I can't ask the witches for help until I'm a full member of the Charmed Circle."

"I don't understand why you can't ask them anyway," Tom said as he put the plate in the sink. "They seem very nice. They send Grandmother flowers every month… So why do you have to be part of the circle? Aren't your witches meant to help people?"

His sister picked up Sparks and began to stroke her. "But Grandmother's not an ordinary person. She's a witch."

"I still don't see—" Tom began, but Tallulah cut him off. "Honestly, Tom. You've got to believe me. This is the only way – and that's why you've got to find out what food they like. We've got hardly any time! I'm relying on you."

Tom took a deep breath. "OK. I'll start tomorrow. How do I get to their houses?"

"On my broomstick, of course," Tallulah said. "You can go just as soon as it's dark."

At breakfast the next morning, Tom noticed the cookbook propped open at the end of the table. His grandmother had always made the meals, so he and Tallulah had never spent any time in the kitchen. Since their grandmother's illness Tallulah had refused to let Tom help her – even when she salted the custard and blackened the sausages, or served half-cooked eggs and raw potatoes, she always had an excuse. "I just need a bit more practice…"

Tom had assumed that she knew what she was doing, but now, looking at the cookbook, he began to wonder.

"Why are you reading that?" Tallulah banged the bread on the table as he turned a page. "I've been looking at it and it's useless!"

"Just a minute…" Tom went on reading. "Macaroni and cheese. Four cups macaroni, one half stick butter, a quarter cup flour, two and a half cups milk. So you're meant to measure the ingredients out? I didn't know that. You just throw things all together any old how, don't you, Lou?"

Tallulah scowled.

"It's called being creative. Those cups and stuff are for people who can't cook."

"But maybe measuring things might make it work better?"

His sister's scowl grew fiercer. "I can do it! I just need to keep on trying. And I thought we were going to have breakfast, not argue about an old cookbook!"

"Can I have a try?" Tom turned over another page. "While we're waiting for it to get dark? There's a recipe here for yummy-looking cookies. If I make some, I could take them to your witches. I could pretend I'm selling them to make money for poor little orphans, and that's true in a way because we are … and then we can have a chat about our favorite foods." He looked up with a beaming smile. "Hey! Don't you think that's a brilliant idea?"

"Mmmmmm…" Tallulah hesitated. "It's OK, I suppose. There's only one thing wrong. You can't cook. I'll make them."

Years of living with a determined older sister had made Tom cunning. "Tell you what. We'll *both* make cookies, and then we'll have enough for all the witches."

Much to his relief, Tallulah laughed. "If you want to play at cooking, I won't stop you. But don't expect me to eat any of the rubbish you make! Now, pass the jam."

Chapter Five

By FIVE O'CLOCK that day the shadows were
growing longer, and Tom had lit the lamps.
The kitchen was full of a wonderful smell of hot
cinnamon and ginger, overlaid by wisps of smoke.
Tallulah smiled proudly as she went to open the
oven door. "There!" she said. "Perfect cookies…"
She pulled out the top tray and reeled back as
she saw the blackened contents. "Oh no! What
happened?"

Wriggling round in front of her, Tom pulled

out a second tray. His cookies were a perfect golden brown. He picked one up and snapped it in two. "Here. Let's try them."

Tallulah ate the cookie slowly. She had expected her brother's attempts to be a disaster, but the cinnamon and ginger mixture was delicious. She licked the last crumbs off her fingers. "Not bad for a beginner. Let's go and try the broomstick." And she headed for the door.

By the time Tom had tried the broomstick three or four times Tallulah was feeling better. However good he was at cooking, there was no doubt he was bad at flying. He could make the broomstick rise in the air, but as soon as his feet left the ground he fell off.

"Ouch!" He rubbed his elbow. "Let's try with the two of us, so I can hang on to you."

Much to Tallulah's surprise, this worked and she was able to show off a few whirls and twirls while Tom clutched her round the waist.

"Wow!" he said as they landed. "You're really good, Lou." He paused. "I don't think I could ever manage a broomstick on my own."

Tallulah looked pleased. "That was good, wasn't it? Tell you what – I'll take you. I can keep out of the way while you knock on the doors. Why don't we visit Miss Dolly first? She's nice, and she was Grandmother's friend."

Tom was happy to agree, and he went to find a box for the cookies while his sister ran down to the garden shed to tell their grandmother they were going out.

As they walked together down the path, Sparks followed them. When Tallulah and Tom climbed onto the broomstick she sprang up behind them, and the broom lifted into the air. Tom held on tightly as his feet left the ground, and gasped as they soared up into the darkness of the night.

"Wheeeeeee!"

Tallulah was jubilant.

"That's my best takeoff ever! I suppose it must be the extra weight."

Tom didn't answer. He had his eyes shut.

"We'll be there in no time," Tallulah went on. "Don't you just love flying, Tom?"

"Ummmm…" was all that Tom could manage,

but Tallulah took this as agreement.

"I'm going to see how fast we can go," she said, and Tom tightened his grip. A moment later he felt his hair lift as they flew faster and faster, then faster still.

"*MEEEOW!* Slow down!" Sparks, balanced on the bristles, dug her claws into Tom's back, but Tom was beyond noticing. Tallulah was talking to him but he couldn't hear a word, and it wasn't until they landed with a soft thump that his ears began to work again.

"Wow!" Tallulah climbed off the broomstick and stretched. "Wasn't that amazing? And look … that must be Miss Dolly's cottage over there behind the trees."

Tom sat down. His legs were too wobbly to hold him up. He opened and shut his mouth, but no words came out.

Tallulah looked at him. "What's the matter?"

"That was … that was the scariest thing I've

ever done," he said. "I NEVER want to go that fast again, Lou. Never ever."

Tallulah sighed. "Oh well. We'll go home slower."

Tom shook his head. "I'm walking."

"Don't be silly. You wouldn't get back until tomorrow. Now, are you ready? You've got cookies to deliver!"

Chapter Six

AFTER TALLULAH HAD, much to his indignation, insisted on smoothing Tom's hair and straightening his spectacles, he took the box of cookies out of his pocket and set off. He was pleasantly surprised to find the path was lined with rosebushes; their scent hung in the air, and the moonlight turned the petals silver.

The cottage, when he reached it, was even more welcoming. The freshly painted front door had a cheery brass sunflower for a knocker, and there was a golden glow from the windows. A large fluffy cat with magnificent whiskers was sitting on the doorstep, and as Tom bent down to stroke her she looked at him with big green eyes.

"Have you come to see Miss Dolly, lovey?" she asked. "I heard you coming up the path." She licked her lips. "I can smell something deeeeelicious in that box you're carrying!"

"Erm," Tom began, but at that moment the front door flew open.

"A visitor! How lovely!" Miss Dolly's round pink face beamed at him. "And you've met my darling Fluffikins! I hope she made you welcome?"

Fluffikins wound round and round Miss Dolly's legs, purring loudly. "Ask him what he's got in that box, lovey," she said. "It smells yummy yummy yummy!"

"Really, Fluffikins. Where are your manners?" Miss Dolly nodded at Tom. "Do excuse her! And please come in. Would you like a cup of tea?"

Tom followed Miss Dolly into her little sitting room. Every chair, sofa and lampshade was patterned with different-colored roses, and for a moment he wondered if he'd walked into a garden. Miss Dolly saw his expression and laughed. "I do so love roses!"

"The roses on the path are lovely," Tom said politely. He held out the box of cookies and took a deep breath. He wasn't good at lying. "I brought you these. I ... I'm collecting for charity."

Miss Dolly put her head to one side, her blue eyes very bright. "You are, are you, dear? And what charity would that be?"

"Oh!" Tom was taken by surprise. "Orphans. That is—"

"Goodness!" Miss Dolly interrupted him with a squeak of delight. "I've seen that box before! I gave it to my dear friend Tabitha last Christmas! Look…" She turned the box round, and to his horror Tom saw a small label: *Dearest Tabitha, with love from Dolly.*

"Yes," he said. "So it does…"

Miss Dolly clapped her hands. "I do believe I've guessed! You must be Tabitha's grandson. She told me Tallulah had a brother … but I don't remember your name."

For a moment Tom had the wild idea of denying any knowledge of either Tallulah or his grandmother, but something about Miss Dolly's sharp eyes made him think it was best to tell the truth. "Yes," he said, "I'm Tom."

"I'm delighted to meet you, dear. And how is your grandmother? Is she feeling better? Do tell me she is! I miss her very much." Miss Dolly gave him a sideways glance. "So strange that she was taken ill like that. I do sometimes wonder whether there might be something a little suspicious about it… But perhaps I'm being foolish. Have you come with a message from her?"

"Not … not exactly a message," Tom said.

Fluffikins jumped onto the arm of Miss Dolly's chair and put a paw on her arm. "Open the cookies, lovey! I can't wait any longer."

Miss Dolly shook her finger at the cat. "Now now, Fluffikins! Don't be greedy." She took out a cookie, nibbled the edge … and her eyes shone. "Oh my goodness me," she said. "Tabitha IS better. Nobody makes cookies like she does … oh happy happy HAPPY day!" And she enveloped Tom in a soft and lavender-smelling embrace.

Tom felt most uncomfortable. As Miss Dolly let him go he stood first on one foot, and then the other. "I'm so sorry," he said. "I really am … but I made the cookies. Not Grandmother. She … she's still in bed."

Fluffikins gave a small sad meow, and Miss Dolly sank down on her flowery sofa. "Still in bed? That's not good."

"No," Tom agreed. Miss Dolly was looking so sympathetic that he couldn't help adding, "Could you help her?"

Miss Dolly sighed, and shook her head. "I'm so sorry, dear. Even if a full member of the circle asks for help, all the witches have to work together. I've thought of trying many times, but I know Gertrude wouldn't agree if I ask. She and I ... well. That's just the way she is."

Fluffikins put a large furry paw on his knee. "Cookies," she said earnestly. "Eat a cookie, lovey. Nothing like a cookie for chasing away worries, and helping you think. 'Empty tum, brain numb.' That's what I always say."

Miss Dolly gazed fondly at her cat. "She's SUCH a clever puss. Here, Fluffikins! A cookie for you." She looked back at Tom. "You're a good cook, young man. Not like your poor sister."

Tom nodded. He was pleased the conversation had turned to cooking, but as he tried to think of a tactful way to find out Miss Dolly's favorite food, Fluffikins winked at him and began to purr. "She won't have any trouble cooking our favorite dish for the Midnight Feast, will she, lovey? It's the

simplest thing in the world. Tuna casserole. Yummy yummy … and easy peasy peasy!"

Miss Dolly shook her head at Fluffikins, but she was smiling. "Naughty puss! You know I'm not meant to tell anyone."

Fluffikins twitched her long whiskers. "You aren't, lovey. You haven't said a word! You never mentioned that all you have to do is mix tuna and pasta, grate a little cheese on top, and pop it in the oven. *Meeeeow!* I'd like another cookie. Talking of food always makes my tum tum rumble."

Miss Dolly inspected Tom. "You're very like your grandmother, you know," she said. "Have you ever considered witchcraft?"

"Me?" Tom said in surprise. "Lou's the one who wants to be a witch, not me."

"I'd say you might well have a talent for magic, dear." Miss Dolly patted his arm. "Just you wait and see. It might come in handy … you've got a difficult task ahead of you."

"Oh! Have you guessed what I'm doing?" Tom asked.

"Of course we have. You want to help your sister find out the witches' favorite foods." 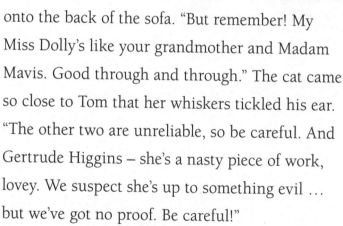 Fluffikins jumped onto the back of the sofa. "But remember! My Miss Dolly's like your grandmother and Madam Mavis. Good through and through." The cat came so close to Tom that her whiskers tickled his ear. "The other two are unreliable, so be careful. And Gertrude Higgins – she's a nasty piece of work, lovey. We suspect she's up to something evil … but we've got no proof. Be careful!"

Tom stood up. "Thank you. You've both been really kind."

Miss Dolly gave him a sad smile. "Anything to

help darling Tabitha, Tom dear. I give Gertrude a bunch of my roses to take to her every month, of course, but I do wish I could do more. Give her my love. Our circle isn't the same without her … not at all. And we wish you and your sister all the luck in the world."

"Come again soon, lovey." Fluffikins licked her paws carefully to check for crumbs. "And bring cookies. Lots of cookies!"

Chapter Seven

TOM WAS FEELING pleased with himself as he walked back down the path. "Tuna casserole," he murmured. "Surely even Lou can manage that. Or I could help her. In fact…" The idea bounced into his head and he wondered why he hadn't thought of it before, "I could do all the cooking!"

Tallulah was waiting for him, Sparks by her side. "You've been ages," she said, and she sounded cross. "Whatever were you doing?"

"Miss Dolly chose tuna casserole," Tom said, unable to keep a note of pride out of his voice. "And guess what, Lou? I might have a talent for magic! Miss Dolly told me after she'd discovered who I was. She says she misses Grandmother terribly, and she really, really hopes she'll get better…" He stopped. His sister wasn't looking at him. She had buried her face in Sparks' fur.

I've said something wrong, he thought. *Oh no…*

"Aren't you clever, Tom Tickle," Tallulah said, and there was an edge to her voice. "I suppose you and your new best friend Miss Dolly are going to make Grandmother better all by yourselves. Perhaps it should be you who joins the Charmed Circle, and you can be the first-ever boy witch and you won't need me at all…" She gave a half-suppressed sob as she fished wildly in her pocket. "No hankie," she sniffed. "Oh rats and bats and *BOTHERATION!*"

Tom got out his own handkerchief to offer his sister, but seeing how dirty it was he pushed it back in his pocket. "I'm sorry, Lou. Did I do it all wrong?"

"Don't be so RIDICULOUS." His sister's face was scarlet. "You found out her favorite meal, didn't you? So of course it wasn't wrong! But how do you think I feel? I've been waiting here wondering if you were being turned into a frog, and I couldn't do anything about it, and then you come skipping back all pleased with yourself and you never even ask me if I'm all right."

Tom climbed silently onto the broomstick, and Sparks jumped on behind him. Tallulah swung her little party up into the air and turned the broomstick towards the small hill that overlooked Miss Dolly's cottage.

That's not the way home, Tom thought. *What's she doing?*

There was no
doubt that Tallulah's
flying skills had
improved. The flight
was smooth, and they
landed neatly in a small hollow. "There," Tallulah
said, and she pointed towards a cluster of twisted
willow trees. "If you go through those, and
then on to the road on the other side, you'll see
Leonora Danglefin's house. If you're so magic,
you might as well see her while we're in the area."
She gave Tom a strange look, half-angry and half-
wistful. "What else did Miss Dolly say? Apart
from you being magic, that is. I don't want to hear
about that."

"She said something that surprised me,"
Tom said slowly. "And Fluffikins did too. They
both seemed to think there was something a bit
suspicious about Grandmother being ill …
but they didn't say what."

"Really?" Tallulah was interested. "Did they think it was a spell of some kind?"

"They didn't say anything about spells," Tom began, and then stopped. "Shh! What's that noise?"

Tallulah glanced round. "I can't hear anything. What is it?"

"Singing," Tom whispered. He put his finger to his lips and pointed upward. There, outlined against the dark night sky, was a figure on a broomstick. Tallulah and Tom froze, and Sparks slipped under Tallulah's cloak. Hardly daring to breathe, they listened as the quavering voice came nearer and nearer.

"Toast the toad and baste the bat,
Mash the mouse tails, roast the rat,
Steam the snails and slice the slugs,
Don't forget to boil the bugs.
Prick a pimple with a pin –
Leonora Danglefin!"

It was, for an achingly long moment,
immediately above their heads, but finally it faded
into the distance.

"Wow," Tom breathed. "Two minutes earlier
and we'd have crashed straight into her!"

Tallulah swallowed. "I know." And then she
scrambled to her feet. "Oh, Tom! You know what
that means, don't you? Her house will be empty."

A cold hand clutched at Tom's stomach.
"Ummmm…"

"You can go and look round! See if you can
find her cookbook in the kitchen." Tallulah's eyes
were shining. "The page that's messiest will be her

favorite. It's easy!"

Tom gulped. "It might sound easy to you, Lou – but what if she comes back and finds me there?"

"Then you'll have to make up a story about being lost," his sister said firmly. "Don't you see? It's a brilliant chance and we've got to take it."

"But it's not 'we,'" Tom protested. "It's me!"

Tallulah's face darkened. "I thought you said you'd help. I'd go if I could – you know I would. But I can't."

Tom was wishing he was safely at home; the thought of creeping around a witch's house made his stomach churn in the most uncomfortable way, and he felt sick. "I'm sorry, Lou."

"It's no good whining," his sister snapped. "Go and do something helpful."

Chapter Eight

LEONORA DANGLEFIN'S house was tall and thin, and surrounded by prickly bushes. The path was narrow and sharp-thorned brambles caught at Tom as he tiptoed nervously towards the front door. His suggestion that Tallulah come with him – after all, Leonora Danglefin was away – had been met with a sarcastic snort, and a reminder that the witch might return at any moment.

Tallulah had then sat herself down under a tree, and started to pull a pinecone to pieces. She hadn't answered when Tom said goodbye.

"Go to the back door," said a voice, and Tom

found Sparks was close behind him. He nodded, and Sparks pattered ahead of him until she came to a sudden stop. "Here we are. I'll look through the window." She leapt up to the window ledge, but after peering through the glass she jumped back, shaking her head.

"Storeroom," she said. "Go and try the door, and see if it's open."

"OK," Tom said, and with infinite caution he crept to the back door and tried the handle. "It's locked."

"Only to be expected," Sparks told him. "Look under the mat."

Tom's heart was thumping as he picked up the large iron key. "I … I suppose I'd better go inside…"

"Hurry up." Sparks' whiskers were twitching. "We don't know how long she's going to be away."

This made Tom's heart beat even harder. His fingers were shaking as he put the key in the lock and turned it. With a loud creak the door swung open, and Tom found himself looking down a long narrow corridor, dimly lit by a row of lamps. It was spotlessly clean and there was such a strong smell of disinfectant that he began to cough.

"Hush!" Sparks glared at him. "You're about to burgle a witch's house. Be quiet! And take off your shoes."

Tom did as he was told, and tiptoed down the corridor. The first three doors were nothing more than small cupboards, but the fourth was half open … and as Tom peeped cautiously in, he saw he'd found the kitchen.

It was immaculately tidy. Everything was neatly lined up, and even the bunches of herbs had been trimmed to exactly the same length.

"Wow!" Tom breathed, remembering the chaos at home. "Now to find the cookbooks!"

At first it seemed as if Leonora didn't have any, but at last Tom spotted a bookshelf high above the precisely stacked saucepans. "She must be very tall," he muttered. "How on earth am I going to reach up there?"

A sudden squawk made him jump. Swinging round, he saw a small cage in a corner. Inside was a crow, its black feathers tattered and its head bald. Tom looked at it anxiously.

"Hello," he said. "Erm … can you talk?"

The crow put its head to one side. "If there be anyone worth talking to, then I do likes to have a natter."

"Oh." Tom gulped. Surely the bird would tell Leonora that he'd broken into her house! He felt even more nervous and began to stammer. "I'm s-s-s-sorry... I lost my way, and I was wondering if anyone here could help me—"

"Liar." The crow hunched itself up. "You be up to something. I can tell, sure as my name's Gargle. What was you after? A magic spell? You'll not be finding any of them round these here parts. Keeps 'em locked away, she do, safe and sound and out of the sight of sharp young lads as might be fancying a bag of gold, or one of them never-ending porridge pots."

Tom shook his head. "I'm not looking for anything. Like I said, I lost my way ... so thank you very much, and I'll go now."

Gargle peered at him. "But you knows as the

lady of the house do be
a witch?"

"Yes ... I mean, is she?"
But Tom wasn't quick
enough, and the crow
began to laugh.

"Caught you out, me
hearty, caught you out!
If you was lost in the woods
for real, you'd have been gawping
and gasping, 'SPELLS? A WITCH?
That's scary, Mr. Gargle!' Now ain't that the case?"

"Yes." Tom was feeling worse and worse. He'd
made a complete mess of his mission, and all
that was left was to tell Tallulah that he'd been
discovered. He gave the row of cookbooks a
sorrowful glance and headed for the door.

"Hold your horses, matey! Hold your horses!"
The crow was clinging to the bars of his cage.
"You and me, me hearty, we could do a deal, see.

Something for you, and something for Mr. Gargle … what d'you say?"

Tom paused. Desperation made him ask, "What kind of deal?"

Gargle winked at him. "Now we's talking! What was it you was after, my ol' buckaroo. Saw you peeping at them books up there, my daisy… thinking they was spell books, was you?"

"No." Tom pushed his spectacles up his nose while he decided what to say. Could he trust the crow? He glanced through the open door to see if Sparks was anywhere near, but there was no sign of her. "Ummmm…" he said slowly. "I was … I was trying to find out what witches eat for their dinner."

"Won't do, matey, won't do. If you was wanting Mr. Gargle on your team, you needs to do better than that."

With a sigh, Tom began to explain. He was expecting Gargle to mock his story, but the moment he mentioned Tallulah the crow began to laugh so hard he had to sit on the floor of his cage to recover his breath.

"Oh, matey!" He wiped his eyes with his wing. "Oh, matey mine! That there sister of yours do be the best. Made me laugh for the first time in weeks and weeks, she did. Made the old dames fall in a bramble bush. Crash bang wallop – down they went! Laugh? I nearly died. Paid for it later, o' course. That Leonora Danglefin – she was spitting nails. Shut me in here and says as I'm not to come out, 'Until you've learned respect, Gargle – respect for your elders and betters.' Betters? BETTERS? I think not. So, my hearty, does us have a deal?"

Tom blinked. "I'm not sure I understand…"

"*Awk!*" Gargle gave a squawk of exasperation. "Let me out of here, young shaver. Let me out, and Mr. Gargle'll help you all he can." His eyes had a wicked gleam. "See if together us can get your sister what she needs." And he rattled the metal bars of his cage.

"I'll let you out. But before I do, can I ask you something?" Tom said. "If you don't like Leonora, why haven't you flown away?"

"Aaark!" The crow lifted up one scaly leg and Tom saw a silver ring round the bird's ankle. "Ties me to her shoulder, she does. Thinks it makes her look smart. Tries to impress that 'orrible Higgins, but it don't work. Higgins is the nastiest piece of witchery I've ever had the misfortune to meet – and Mr. Gargle's met a few down and dirty villains in his time, believe you me."

This was the last thing Tom wanted to hear, but he was also pleased the crow wanted to help. He bent down to open the cage, but Gargle held up a warning wing. "Not so fast, matey, not so fast. Gotta make it look like a break out." And he began to rock the cage to and fro until it fell on the stone floor with a crash, denting it badly. "Now, bend them bars," he ordered. "Bend them open."

This was easier
said than done.
The elegant bars
of the cage were much stronger than they looked;
Tom had to wrap his handkerchief round his
hand to get a firm grip. He was breathless by the
time he had made a gap wide enough for Gargle
to squeeze through.

The crow flew to his shoulder and nibbled his
ear. "You done good, me lad," he said. "And here's
a question. What d'you answer to?"

"Sorry?" Tom looked blank.

"Yer moniker. Label. Tag.
Whatever they calls you."

"Oh!" Light dawned.
"My name's Tom."

"Well, Tom –
watch this!" And the
crow flew straight at
the window. The glass
smashed and a gust of chilly
air swirled round the room.

As Gargle flew back to Tom's shoulder, he was
looking pleased with himself. "There we goes and
there she blows! And I can tell you just what she'll
say: 'Oh, that naughty, naughty crow! Look at the
horrid, horrid mess he's made!'" He inspected the
broken window, his eyes thoughtful. "H'mmm…"
Twisting his head round, he plucked two feathers
from his back. "Setting the scene good and
proper, we are," he remarked, and dropped them
on the floor to lie among the broken splinters of

glass. "So what's the plan now, matey mine? Time to make a sharp exit?"

Tom shook his head. "I've got to find out what Leonora Danglefin's favorite meal is."

"AAAAARK!" Gargle was close by Tom's ear. "Hang on…" He soared into the air and landed on top of the cookbooks. With a well-judged kick, he sent them tumbling to the ground; as they fell, a piece of paper floated out and landed at Tom's feet. Picking it up, he studied it – then grinned an enormous grin. "I think this is it," he said. "Well done, Mr. Gargle! Look! It says, 'A special recipe for Midnight Feasts and other celebrations—'"

"Sssssh!" The crow was listening intently. "Time to go, young fellow-me-lad. Shove that paper back … no, under the books. Now – RUN!"

Tom ran, Gargle speeding ahead of him. They shot out of the back door and Tom snatched up his shoes. Sparks was waiting for them.

"Quick!" she hissed. "She's nearly here!"

With trembling hands, Tom turned the key and dropped it back under the mat. The three of them buried themselves in the bushes surrounding the house.

They were only just in time. Half a minute later Leonora Danglefin came swooping down and, to the watchers' surprise, she was not alone. A second witch was following her, and as Tom peered through the leaves he saw it was a small mousy-looking woman.

"Come in, Dulcie," Leonora said, as the two landed by the back door. "Jam roly-poly pudding, you say? I'm sure there's a picture somewhere in my recipe books. I'll show you." She stooped to collect the key. "Never touch it myself. Much too fattening. 'A moment on the lips, a lifetime on the hips,' is what my mother used to say."

Dulcie gave a weak giggle. "So that's how you keep so wonderfully slim, Leonora. But jam roly-poly was all I could think of, and I don't even know what it looks like. I won't know if Tallulah's got it right or wrong when we have our lovely Midnight Feast."

Leonora gave her friend a superior smile. "We may never have a feast." She held the door open, then pulled Dulcie back. "Shoes off, if you please. I suspect Tallulah Tickle will fail miserably. A nice enough girl, but her cooking skills are truly pathetic..." Her voice died away as she followed Dulcie into the house and shut the door behind her.

Tom looked round at Sparks and Gargle with an enormous grin. "How

lucky was that? Jam roly-poly for Dulcie. We've almost got it all! Should we go now?"

"Surely should, me hearties," Gargle agreed, and Sparks slipped away like a little black shadow. Tom was about to head after her when he heard a scream … a scream that made his ears tingle.

Leonora Danglefin was in her kitchen.

Chapter Nine

TALLULAH had also heard the scream. As Sparks and Tom came running towards her, Gargle flying above them, she scrambled to her feet, clutching her broomstick in case a speedy escape was required.

"It's OK, Lou," Tom gasped. "They didn't see us. And we've got brilliant news!"

Tallulah didn't answer. She was staring in alarm at the crow. "That's Leonora's bird!" Her face was pale. "Tom – what have you done? He'll tell her about us!"

"No, he won't," Tom said, and Gargle landed on

Tallulah's shoulder with a caw of delight.

"Mr. Gargle at your service, Miss Tallulah. Owes you the biggest laugh of my life, I do, and that's a fact." He gave a hoarse chuckle. "So

you ask Mr. Gargle for anything you wants, anything at all."

"Ummmm ... thank you." Tallulah, recovered from her fright, turned to Tom and Sparks. "Did you kidnap him?"

Gargle looked offended. "Me? Ain't nobody sharp enough to kidnap this old bird! Nah. Got a deal, we have. Going to see you gets your wish, Miss Tallulah, and gets it soon."

"We know what Dulcie wrote down," Tom said eagerly. "It's jam roly-poly pudding! And I'm sure Leonora chose broomstick pie."

"Broomstick pie? What's that?" Tallulah asked.

"Just an ordinary apple pie, but you leave stalks of rosemary sticking through the pastry so they look like little broomsticks. It's her mother's recipe."

"*Pssst!*" Gargle was listening, his head to one side. "I hears voices."

Neither Tallulah nor Tom could hear anything, but Sparks whispered, "The witches … one of them's leaving. She'll be airborne any minute."

There was a faint *whoooooosh!* in the night sky as Dulcie flew away, a large cookbook under her arm. Tom counted to ten before he said, "She should be out of earshot by now."

"I'd say we needs to get a move on," Gargle suggested. "That Leonora – she'll be out any minute looking for me."

"Should we try to visit Gertrude Higgins?" Tom asked, but Tallulah shook her head.

"It's late. We ought to get home. We can't leave Grandmother too long." She paused. "You've done all right, Tom. That's four out of the five. I'll start cooking in the morning so everything's ready for the day after. And I'll take you to Gertrude's house tomorrow evening; she doesn't live far away."

"I was thinking I could help," Tom began, but Tallulah cut him off.

"Just because you were lucky with those cookies doesn't mean you can cook. I'm the one who's going to be a witch, remember – and it's me that's going to save Grandmother. Especially as I'm beginning to think your Miss Dolly was right … there's something strange going on. It's best if you leave everything to me."

Tom opened his mouth to protest, then thought better of it. He climbed obediently onto the broomstick and Sparks jumped on behind him. "Very wise," she said in his ear.

Gargle settled himself on Tom's shoulder. "Save the old wings," he said. "Why bother to fly when you can ride?"

The flight home was not as speedy as the flight out had been, and Tom had almost begun to enjoy himself by the time they were circling above their cottage.

"Class flying," Gargle remarked as they landed without so much as a bump, and Tallulah grinned before she and Tom headed for the garden shed to check on their grandmother.

As they opened the door, they noticed a sickly smell. Tallulah was first inside, and Tom heard her give a gasp of horror. "Oh no!"

Anxiously he peered over her shoulder. His grandmother was back in her bed, but the yellow scales had crept up her arms and her fingers were curled into claws. Pink smoke hung thickly around her and she was clearly breathing it in.

"Open the door wider, Tom," Tallulah instructed. "Let the smoke out!" As Tom did as he was told, their grandmother opened her eyes.

"Pinkie pie," she said. "Don't let the badgers go!

They'll crack the china and curdle the custard…"
She began to sneeze, and Tallulah moved the
flowers away from the bedside so she could hand
her grandmother a handkerchief.

"Thank you, dear." Tabitha's change of tone
was so remarkable that Tom jumped. "Been out
and about, have you?"

Tallulah smiled at her grandmother as she put
the flowers back. "Yes! I'm going to make you
better. But there's something I have to ask you …
what does Gertrude Higgins like eating best?"

"Gertrude?" The smile faded and Tabitha's eyes
dimmed. "Gertie, Gertie, Gertie … got her dress
all dirty…" She sank back on her pillows.

"Please, Grandmother," Tallulah begged.
"Gertrude Higgins … she's one of the witches."
She pointed to the flowers. "One of the Chumley
Charmed Circle! Your friends … you must
remember them. They sent you those."

"It's no good," Tom said sadly. "She's asleep."

He picked up the vase and inspected the contents. "These aren't roses, are they, Lou?"

"Of course not. They're … I'm not sure what they are." Tallulah looked more closely at the deep-purple flowers. "Madam Mavis said they come from Miss Dolly's garden. She sends them every month."

"But Miss Dolly grows roses," Tom began – then he sneezed and interrupted himself. "*ATCHOOOO!*" A frantic search of his pockets produced no handkerchief, and he was forced to wipe his nose on his sleeve.

"That's disgusting," Tallulah told him.

Tom shrugged. "Sorry – I must have lost my hankie."

"Don't worry about it." Tallulah heaved an enormous sigh. "Come on, Tom. It's time for bed."

"Cheer up!" Tom gave his sister an encouraging pat on the back. "If we do as well tomorrow as we did today, you'll be a proper witch in no time."

"Let's hope so," Tallulah said. "We haven't got much time, and I have a feeling something's bound to go wrong."

If Tallulah had been able to see Leonora Danglefin, she would have known she was right. The witch was storming round her kitchen

holding a grubby
handkerchief,
embroidered
with the initials T.T.
"T.T. – that has to be
Tallulah Tickle. But how
did it get here? Surely she
didn't come here to help
that horrible bird?" She
shook her head, then froze
as a new idea struck her.
"OH! I know what she
was doing. Of course … The
cookbooks. She was looking for my recipes!"

Leonora put the handkerchief in her pocket
and sank into a chair, her expression cunning.
"Well, well, well… Should I tell darling Gertrude?
Or Madam Mavis? H'mmm … let me think."

She leaned her head on her hand while she
tried to decide what would be best for her future

as a member of the Charmed Circle. She admired
Madam Mavis, but she knew all too well that if
she upset Gertrude Higgins there'd be no end to
the itches and rashes.

"I'll tell Gertrude," she decided. "I'll go and see
her tonight."

Chapter Ten

TOM WAS UP early the following morning. Leaving Gargle asleep on the top of the wardrobe, he hurried downstairs to find Tallulah already in the kitchen. She was standing at the table, looking even more determined than usual.

"You'll have to get your own breakfast," she told Tom. "I'm making an apple pie."

Tom looked at the heap of apples on the table and whistled. "Wow!"

"Tomorrow's the Midnight Feast," Tallulah said. "But you don't need to worry. I'll get lots done today." She picked up a bag of flour and

tipped it into a bowl. "And anyone can make an apple pie, so I thought I'd start with that."

"I'll take Grandmother her tea," Tom said. As he put the kettle on to boil, he watched Tallulah mixing the flour with salt and water then stir hard. He glanced at the closed cookbook. "Is that what it says to do?"

Tallulah glared at him. "I've told you! I know what I'm doing. Don't you trust me?"

Tom found this difficult to answer. He had complete faith in his sister's strength of character, but not in her cooking methods.

He pushed his glasses up his nose. "You know what, Lou? I'm absolutely certain that if anyone can save Grandmother, it'll be you."

When Tom took Grandmother her tea and toast she was back on her shelf. She was pleased to see him, however, and asked him if he had changed his socks. Taking this as a good sign, Tom asked her about Gertrude Higgins, but all he got in reply was a loud snort and a suggestion to "twiddle your thumbs and play on a parsnip."

As Tom left the shed, Sparks was sunning herself on the garden wall. "Hello," he said. "How are you?"

Sparks stretched out a paw, inspected it, then began to clean between her toes. She didn't answer, and Tom stood watching her, wondering if she was going to say anything. A thought came to him. "You were Grandmother's cat before she was ill, weren't you?"

Sparks looked up. "Of course. And I'd prefer to be described as a companion, if you don't mind."

Tom leaned against the wall. "Sorry. So you've been to loads of meetings… What's Gertrude Higgins like?"

"Evil." Sparks' tail began to twitch. "She's one of the old-style witches. And she wants to be the leader of the Circle."

"I always thought all witches were good," Tom said, "just like Grandmother."

"Well, they aren't." Sparks shook her head. "Some are good. Some just follow along. And some are bad. Very bad."

"So what'll happen if Gertrude does get to be leader?" Tom wanted to know.

"She'll bring back Black Magic – and then nobody will be safe!" Sparks hissed before jumping off the wall and running back to the cottage. Tom scratched his ear thoughtfully, then hurried after her.

Tallulah was still in the kitchen, flour in her hair, surrounded by pans, open bags, apple peelings and scrappy pieces of gray pastry. There was a strange smell in the air, and Tom looked doubtfully at the oven. "Is your apple pie all right, do you think?"

His sister's eyes flashed, but before she could answer Gargle came flapping into the kitchen and landed heavily on her shoulder. "Morning, me hearties all," he said. "Mmmmm … cooking, are we? Gotta bite or two for a hungry bird, Miss Tallulah?"

"The pie's not ready yet," Tallulah said. She didn't sound welcoming, but she managed a faint smile for the crow. "Tom'll make you a piece of toast. Just don't get in my way – I've got to make a jam roly-poly pudding."

"Roly-poly, pudding and pie!" Gargle clicked his beak enthusiastically. "Go, girl, go!" He flew over to Tom. "Shake a leg there, matey mine!

Toast's a tasty treat for an old sailor like yours truly. Make it hot, mind – and I don't want no burnt edges!"

After breakfast, the day went from bad to worse. Tallulah's apple pie was a disaster. The apples bubbled from under the gray crust and dribbled out of the oven onto the kitchen floor. She told Tom to clean up while she finished her jam roly-poly, and when he tasted the pie he discovered the apples were sour enough to make his tongue curl and the pastry was salty. *She's muddled up the salt and sugar again*, he thought, but he didn't dare say anything. The atmosphere in the kitchen was already thunderous.

The roly-poly was just as much of a failure. It wouldn't roll up, and when Tallulah

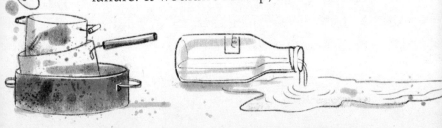

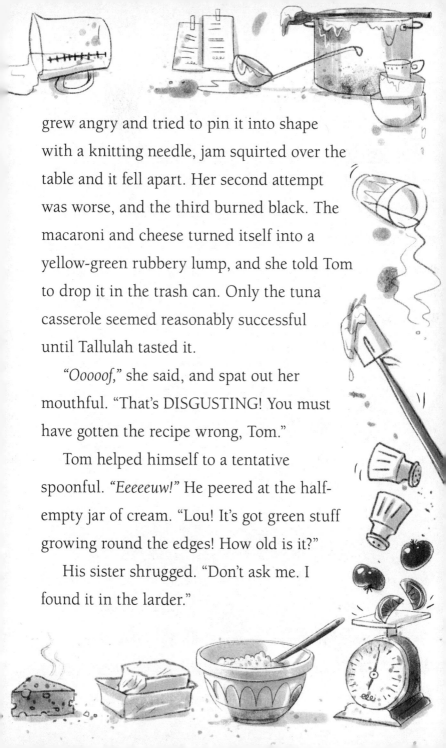

grew angry and tried to pin it into shape with a knitting needle, jam squirted over the table and it fell apart. Her second attempt was worse, and the third burned black. The macaroni and cheese turned itself into a yellow-green rubbery lump, and she told Tom to drop it in the trash can. Only the tuna casserole seemed reasonably successful until Tallulah tasted it.

"*Ooooof,*" she said, and spat out her mouthful. "That's DISGUSTING! You must have gotten the recipe wrong, Tom."

Tom helped himself to a tentative spoonful. "*Eeeeeuw!*" He peered at the half-empty jar of cream. "Lou! It's got green stuff growing round the edges! How old is it?"

His sister shrugged. "Don't ask me. I found it in the larder."

"You could have killed someone!" Tom was so horrified he forgot to be tactful. Gargle, who had been watching the morning's activities with interest, cackled loudly. "That's my girl! Feed the Higgins poison! Send her reeling. That'll settle her hash."

Tom held his breath and waited for Tallulah to explode, but she didn't. She collapsed onto a chair, put her head on the messy table and burst into floods of tears. "I knew I couldn't do it, I knew it! But I wanted SO MUCH to be able to make Grandmother better and I can't…" Her sobs overcame her and she couldn't say any more.

Not knowing what else to do, Tom fetched her

a glass of water. "It's OK, Lou. It'll be all right..."

"No it WON'T!" Tallulah roared. "It'll NEVER be all right and Grandmother'll turn into a chicken and fly away and I'll spend the rest of my life looking after you and the house and it'll be awful, awful, AWFUL! *Boohoooo … boohooooooo … boohooooo…*"

Tom looked at Sparks, who was sitting on the windowsill, but the little cat had no advice to give. It was Gargle who came to the rescue. As Tallulah's sobs lessened he hopped forward, careful to avoid the jam.

"*AAARK!* Listen here, me hearties. Seems to me there's a right old fuss going on about nothing at all." He pointed at Tallulah with a tattered wing.

"No good at cooking? So what! You've got other skills, you have, Miss T. You be a witch, don't you? And what do witches do? They makes things happen. Right? But do they do the dirty work themselves? Not on your nelly! They points their wand, and boooooof! It's done! Now you ain't got no wand. So point your finger! Point it at that brother of yours. Tell him, 'Make me jam roly-polies by the dozen!' Abracadabra! Far as I remember, all you has to do is bring a Midnight Feast that fits the bill. Am I right, or am I right?"

Tallulah lifted her head from the table and stared at him. "You're right," she said slowly. "And I've just thought of something. Grandmother never spent much time in the kitchen. She waved her wand and dinners floated onto the table … so maybe she couldn't cook either! It all makes sense… I'm like her!"

"There you is." Gargle looked smug. "I'm

a wise old bird, I am. Now, wipe that jam
off your chinny chin chin and let's get the show
on the road."

"Yes!" Tallulah leapt up from the table. "Guess
what, Tom? We're going to do things differently.
We're going to be a team!"

Tom looked hopeful. "So do I get to do the
cooking?"

"Of course," his sister said loftily. "You can start
right now. I'm going to sit with Grandmother and
have a rest. I'm worn out." She took off her apron

and handed it to her brother. "Here! You've got ages until we leave for Gertrude's house."

Tom looked at the messy table as Tallulah marched off. Thinking about the evening ahead, he shivered. "I really, REALLY don't want to go there. But I suppose I must."

Chapter Eleven

LEONORA DANGLEFIN'S news had infuriated Gertrude Higgins. She had woken early and was striding up and down her garden, muttering to herself. "So Tallulah Tickle's been sneaking into Leonora's kitchen! Ha! Will she dare to come here, I wonder? I'll be ready for her if she does. What shall I give her, Kibble? Snakes instead of hair? Rabbit ears? Hooves and a tail?"

Kibble didn't answer. Gertrude had been too distracted by Leonora's visit to notice that he had eaten the crusts from her cheese sandwich, and he was anxiously waiting for the moment when she did.

Gertrude went on muttering. "No … no. There's an opportunity here … an opportunity to show Mavis that even if the girl does get a few meals right, it's only because she's been peeking and prying. But how best to do it? Bah!" She kicked at a cabbage and it rolled along the path in front of her. She kicked it again and it landed on a patch of deep-purple flowers, almost hidden by the ivy at the end of the garden. A sickly smell filled the air, and Gertrude hastily put her handkerchief over her nose and headed back to her room. Kibble, eyes watering, hurried after her.

Once inside, Gertrude slammed the door and blew her nose. "Phew! The Agonies are stronger than ever. Excellent … but I'll not pick any today. Today I need to deal with the girl, not her grandmother."

Gertrude blew her nose a second time as she flicked over the pages of her book of spells. "H'mmmm … a spell for spots before the eyes

… dizziness … toad's feet … no. Those won't do. Perhaps something simpler? Aha!" She shut the book with a triumphant bang. "I'll trick her! I'll leave a recipe on my table where she's bound to find it when she comes sneaking round. Let me see … I know. A chocolate birthday cake. When she brings it to the Midnight Feast, Mavis will reveal our choices … and Tallulah Tickle will fail the test because she'll be wrong, wrong, WRONG!"

She cackled gleefully and went to find a cookbook. Opening it at "The Most Delicious Chocolate Cake Ever," she underlined the recipe and scribbled "My favorite! Never fails to delight!" on the margin of the page before placing the open book on the table. "There," she said. "And if – oh, silly, silly, forgetful me – I leave the curtains open and a lamp burning when I go out to see Enid tonight, anyone looking through the window will be able to read it."

Delighted with her own cleverness, she looked round for yesterday's crusts. Finding only an empty plate, her cheery mood fell away, and she stormed towards the trembling Kibble.

By the time the day was fading into evening, Tom had made a sugar-crusted broomstick apple pie, a jam roly-poly oozing strawberry jam, a delicious, golden macaroni and cheese and a mouthwatering tuna casserole.

"That's everything done," he told Sparks and

Gargle, "except for whatever it is that Gertrude Higgins wants."

As he was carefully moving the food to the larder, Tallulah came in coughing.

"How's Grandmother?" Tom asked.

"I couldn't really tell." Tallulah yawned, and coughed again. "She was asleep. Actually—" she looked faintly ashamed of herself—"I had a nap as well… What's the matter?"

Tom was staring at her, his eyes wide. "Lou! There's pink smoke coming out of your nose!"

"What?" Tallulah began to laugh. "That's ridiculous! It's just drifted in with me."

Not entirely reassured, Tom nodded. "If you say so. Hey! I've done loads of cooking. Do you want to see?"

"I'll look later." Tallulah was dismissive. "We should be going." She went to the door and looked out. "Gertrude doesn't live far away, so it'll only be a short flight."

Sparks jumped down from the windowsill, Gargle flapped his way onto Tom's shoulder and the three of them followed Tallulah into the twilight.

The flight began well, but after five minutes or so it began to rain and Tom was soon wet. Sparks crept close to him for warmth, and Gargle muttered darkly in his ear about damp feathers and the dangers of pneumonia. Tallulah, who was wearing her witch's cloak, didn't seem to notice. Her steering was erratic and Tom wondered if she knew where she was going. His suspicions were confirmed when she landed with a thump at the edge of a field and began searching her pockets.

"I've got a map somewhere," she said. "Here it is… Oh. Hang on a moment." She frowned, and turned the map round. "That's better. We're not far away. Tom, you're not being much help – can you keep a proper lookout, please?"

Tom's teeth were chattering with cold as he stared at his sister in astonishment. "Look out for what, exactly?"

"Gertrude's house, of course. It's some kind of tower, and it's near a pond." Tallulah folded up the sodden map and put it back in her pocket. "I thought we were going to work as a team?"

"But you never said to look for a tower," Tom protested.

"Well, I'm saying it now." Tallulah climbed back on her broomstick and Tom climbed on behind her, wishing he was brave enough to tell her she was being unfair.

He squinted into the darkness until a faint gleam down below suggested water, and he pulled at Tallulah's sleeve. "I think that might be the pond."

A swift dive downward proved Tom was right, and once they had landed Tallulah pointed towards a twinkling light. "That must be her house," she said. "Looks as if she's at home. Knock on the door and tell her you're lost, Tom—"

"This old bird's gotta better idea," Gargle interrupted. "I'll go first and have a look-see!" And with a shake of his wet feathers he was off.

Tom crossed his fingers. He was aware that luck had been on his side so far; now, standing under a dripping tree, the idea of facing a truly

evil witch seemed terrifying. A trickle of rain made its way down the back of his neck and he was unable to stop himself sneezing.

"*Shh!*" Tallulah dug him sharply in the ribs. Tom shivered, and tried to think of warm and comfortable things to make himself feel better. Miss Dolly's pretty room floated into his mind, and he imagined her sitting happily in front of her fire, Fluffikins on her knee. *All those roses!* he thought. *I wonder if she ever gets tired of them?*

Something began to worry him. "Roses…" he murmured, and then again, "Roses … oh! Oh … of COURSE!" He pulled at his sister's arm. "Lou. Lou! I've just had an idea! It's Gertrude who brings Grandmother the flowers every month, isn't it? The flowers from the Charmed Circle?"

"Why on earth are you bothering about that now?" Tallulah asked.

"Because they should be *roses* and they're not!" Tom's voice grew loud with excitement, and

Tallulah stared at him through the darkness and the rain.

"*Sssh!* She'll hear you! What do you mean, they should be roses? They're those purple things. You know they are."

Tom swallowed. "I think it's the flowers that are making Grandmother ill. Miss Dolly told me she sends roses, so someone's changing them. And I think it's Gertrude Higgins. It must be some kind of bad spell."

"But members of the Chumley Charmed Circle aren't allowed to use Black Magic!" Tallulah's voice rose. "You can't join unless you promise to help people! I know Gertrude's horrible, but making those kinds of spells is completely evil. You can't be right, Tom."

Tom took a deep breath. "Think about it, Lou. It all makes sense. Gertrude's trying to change Grandmother into a chicken!"

"Maybe." There was an unusual note of doubt

in Tallulah's voice. "Tell you what. We'll look in her garden. We won't wait for Gargle – we'll go right now. And if we find the purple flowers … well, then I might believe you."

Chapter Twelve

IT WAS STILL RAINING as Tom and Tallulah crept towards the crumbling tower, leaving Sparks under the trees. Tom's shoes were soaked through, and his hands and feet were so cold he could hardly feel them. A sudden gust of wind pulled the heavy clouds away from the moon; he had the briefest glimpse of ivy-covered walls, and then it was dark again.

On they went, until a thorny hedge blocked their way. "I can see the gate," Tallulah whispered. "Over there, look. And it's open!"

Together they tiptoed into the garden. The rain was easing, but the wind was blowing more strongly; gaps appeared in the clouds and shafts of moonlight came and went. Tom, crouching low in case anyone was watching from the windows, worked his way slowly down the path. Tallulah stayed close to the wall so she could peer into the stone pots by the door. Something moved in the shadows and she froze … and relaxed again as a large toad hopped away. "Phew," she breathed.

Tom was now at the bottom of the garden. He'd seen nothing unusual, and was beginning to despair when he heard a faint cry.

"*Woooooowl!* Help! Help me! I'm drowning…"

Looking round, Tom saw a wooden water barrel leaning against the fence. It was too dark to see inside, but Tom cautiously put his arm over the rim. Feeling cold wet fur, he snatched it away again. "Hello?" he whispered. "Who's there?"

There was a scrabbling, followed by a splash.

"Help! I'm going to drown!"

Tom put his arm back in, and claws caught his hand. A moment later a soaking-wet cat was shivering on his shoulder.

"You poor thing!" Tom could feel the animal's bones as he stroked him. "You're so thin! Have you been there for ages?"

"The witch threw me in. All I did was eat a crust!" The cat sneezed. "She's evil. If it wasn't for the pies I'd run away … but I want those pies. I'm SO HUNGRY! I'm hollow to the end of my tail."

"So you're Gertrude Higgins' cat?" Tom felt a wave of horror sweep over him. "Oh no! Are you going to tell her I'm here?"

"What?" Kibble, who had begun to clean himself, stopped to stare. "Tell her? I can't. She's out. Besides, I don't tell her anything. She doesn't ever listen to poor old Kibble. Too busy muttering about her plots and plans. Hates me, she does … but she promised me pies and all sorts, and that's worth a lot of kicks and sticks. Do anything for a pie, I would."

Much relieved to hear Gertrude was out, Tom stood up. "Can I ask you something?"

Kibble looked suspicious. "What is it?"

Tom leaned towards him. "Is there anything strange growing here?"

"Can't tell you. Sorry about that. Took the oath, I did… 'A witch's cat never betrays his owner.' Even when she's as mean as my lady. But seeing as you rescued me, I owe you. Look behind the ivy – not that I'm saying there's anything there." And Kibble leapt over the fence into the darkness.

"Tom! Who were you talking to?" Tallulah had come to join him.

"Gertrude's cat," Tom said. "He says to look under the ivy." He went towards the back wall. The ivy was as thick as a heavy curtain; he pushed it to one side with difficulty. There were flowers growing behind, and as Tom peered at them the moon sailed out from behind the clouds. "They're the same as the flowers by Grandmother's bed!" he whispered. "Do you believe me now?"

"I don't know…" Tallulah bent down and picked one. "Yuck! It smells horrible! Let's take it home and see if it really is the same."

Before Tom could answer, there was a flutter of wings and Gargle flew down, his black eyes gleaming. "Wotcher," he said, "I've found the recipe!"

"You found it?" Tallulah jumped back to the path. Tom dropped the ivy and followed her as she hurried back towards the tower.

"Round the back," Gargle said. "This way!"

Tallulah and Tom crept after the crow. Light was shining out of a low window, and as they peered in they could easily read the recipe lying on the table.

"Wow! Chocolate cake! I can make that." Tom's eyes shone, but Tallulah was suddenly doubtful.

"Something doesn't feel right," she said as they made their way back to the gate. "Don't you think it all looks a bit obvious? As if it might be a trick?"

Tom looked at her in surprise. "A trick?"

Tallulah shrugged. "Gertrude's clever. She'd never leave her curtains open by mistake. And would she really choose chocolate cake?"

"*Awk!*" Gargle gazed at Tallulah with admiration. "Reckon as you could be right, Miss T. And she was writing a whole lot more than that on her paper. Brains, that's what you've got. Brains."

"So it's hopeless." Tallulah was trying hard not to cry. "We'll never find out what she chose. And I'll never get to be a proper witch … and Grandmother won't ever get better. Oh Tom! What shall we do?"

"I don't know," Tom said. "Go home? We can check on the flowers. If they're the same we should throw them away. That might help Grandmother."

"I suppose so." Tallulah didn't sound hopeful. "Let's go."

Ten minutes later Gertrude Higgins flew back. As soon as she landed she called for the toad. "So?"

"Girl," he reported. "Want my dinner!"

"Kibble will feed you," Gertrude promised, then cackled loudly. "Well, he will if he's learned to swim!" Still cackling, she walked down to the water barrel. "Kibble? Are you there?"

When there was no answer, Gertrude peered inside. "Surely he couldn't have jumped out?" Footprints in the wet earth caught her attention, and she nodded. "That'll be the girl!" She studied the ivy, but Tom had been careful. "No. No sign she's been snooping there."

Making her way up the path, she found Kibble shivering on the doorstep. She grunted, and kicked him inside before sitting down at her table.

"I had my dinner with Enid," she told him. "You don't deserve anything, so don't go yowling for food."

Kibble drooped, and went to sit in a corner. Gertrude gave him a cold look. "The girl fished you out, did she? Ha! But I've tricked her. And tomorrow night she'll be seen for what she is – a silly little fraud, and she'll be thrown out of the Circle forever!"

Chapter Thirteen

T OM COULDN'T SLEEP. He tossed and turned, his
mind whirling, and not long after midnight he
got up and crept down to the kitchen. After a
moment's hesitation, he opened the back door and
went to the shed. He had thrown away the purple
flowers as soon as they got home, and he was half
hoping his grandmother might be better – but she
was fast asleep. Even when he tried gently shaking
her arm, she didn't stir.

Maybe she'll be better tomorrow, he told himself.

As he walked back to the cottage, a thought
came to him and he stopped to consider it.

I wonder ... should I try? He gave himself a shake. *Yes. I'll go on my own.... so if it doesn't work, Lou won't be disappointed.* And he hurried towards the kitchen.

Gargle was waiting for him. "It's beddy byes time, old pal. What's up?"

"I've had an idea," Tom said. "I'm going to see if I can find Gertrude's cat. He might know what she really chose ... it's our last chance!"

Gargle flapped his wings. "Certainly is."

Tom went to the kitchen cupboards, and took out a pork pie. "Kibble said he'd do anything for one of these ..." He put it in his pajama pocket.

As they went outside, Gargle was astonished to see Tom pick up Tallulah's broomstick. "Oi oi, matey mine!" he said. "What's with the brush?"

"It's too far to walk," Tom said grimly. He climbed onto the broomstick, and Gargle settled on his shoulder. With a sudden lurch they rose upward, then sank down ... and then with a swoop they were up again, Tom clinging on so hard his knuckles were white. Zigzagging wildly, the broomstick lifted over the trees and flew towards Gertrude Higgins' house in a series of jerks and twists. Tom's attempt to land resulted in a crash into a heap of bracken; he got up and propped the broomstick against a tree. "Now," he whispered to Gargle, "let's see if we can find Kibble."

"I'm on it, matey," Gargle said, and he flew towards the ruined tower, now in darkness. Circling round, he could see no sign of the cat; Tom, creeping into the garden, saw Gargle shaking his head as the bird sailed down to join him.

"What do I do now?" Tom whispered. "I thought cats always went out at night!"

Gargle nudged him. "Most do. And what do they do then, me old duck? They howl. And when one of them's howling, they all join in."

Desperation made Tom bold. He put his hands to his mouth and did his best. *"Merrrrrow! Merrrrrow! MERRRRROW!"*

"Try a bit louder," the crow encouraged.

Tom took a deep breath and tried again. *"Merrrroooooow! MERRRRRROOOOW!"*

This time a window opened above them, and the contents of a bucket of water poured down, soaking Tom. *"Oooof!"* He gasped.

"Scram! Hoosh! Scat!" Gertrude's voice echoed in the night. "Kibble – get out there and tell that animal it'll be something worse than water if it makes another SQUEAK!" There was a muffled yowl as she flung Kibble out, followed by a crash as the window was slammed shut.

As Tom wiped the water out of his eyes, he saw Kibble staring at him.

"Kibble!" he whispered. "I was looking for you – I want to talk."

Kibble backed away. "Why?"

"I need to know what Gertrude Higgins chose for her birthday feast."

"Birthday cake." Kibble glanced nervously up at the window over their heads. "That's what it was. Chocolate birthday cake!"

Tom pulled the pork pie out of his pocket. "That's what she wants us to think." He put the pie on the ground. "I brought you this."

"Ooooooooh!" Kibble leapt forward, and the pie

was gone in seconds. Licking his lips, he looked
hopefully at Tom. "Got any more?" When Tom
shook his head, Kibble sighed. "I'll have to wait.
Puddings and pies, she promised me … puddings
and pies. And tomorrow's the day it all begins.
Tomorrow's the Midnight Feast!"

Tom was shivering with cold. "I'll cook you
anything you like if you tell me what she chose…"

"No can do." Kibble came closer. "She'd know

for sure – and she'd catch me, and pull out my whiskers, and twist my tail off. That's if I was lucky!"

His teeth chattering, Tom gave up. "If you change your mind, I promise I'll look after you. Come anytime!"

Kibble didn't answer, but he sighed as he padded away. Tom shook his head sadly, and set off to find the broomstick.

The flight home was even more erratic than the flight out. Gargle gave up trying to stay on Tom's shoulder, and flew beside him as the broomstick bucked and rolled, scraping the tops of fences one minute and swooshing in between tree trunks the next. By the time they got home Tom's arms were aching, and he was hugely relieved to be able to put the broomstick down.

"Time for bed," he told Gargle, and the bird nodded.

"Tell you one thing, matey mine. That cat's got the answer."

"I know," Tom said wearily. "But what's the use? He won't ever tell us."

Gargle flew up to perch on the top of the cupboard. "Never say never, old duck. You did good, looking after that cat, and that'll bounce back. Pops out to surprise you when you're looking the other way, good does."

Chapter Fourteen

DESPITE HIS MIDNIGHT EXCURSION, Tom was up early the next morning.

"What's that you're making?" Tallulah asked as she came into the kitchen.

"Birthday cake," Tom said. "I thought you ought to take one. After all, today's Gertrude's birthday…"

Tallulah sighed. "But she'll still win. And you know what, Tom? Grandmother's still asleep. I've just been to check."

"Sleeping's better than squawking and perching on the end of her bed," Tom told her.

"Maybe." But Tallulah didn't sound hopeful.

In Gertrude Higgins' tower, the mood of the morning was even darker. Gertrude was glowering at the footprints under her bedroom window and, noticing there were paw prints among them, she called for Kibble. "Who was here?" she demanded. "And don't lie, or I'll pull your ears off."

Kibble trembled. "It was a boy," he began.

"Liar!" Gertrude's eyes flashed. "It was that girl, wasn't it? What did you tell her?"

"Nothing!" Kibble cowered down. "Nothing, I swear! I said nothing."

"We'll see about that." The witch seized Kibble by the scruff of the neck and stared into his eyes. "Hah! So you're telling the truth for once! Just remember, Kibble – you swore an oath! You'll be true to me, or—" she smiled a mirthless smile— "I'll make you wish you'd never been born." And she flung him away.

Kibble, quivering against the wall, growled softly to himself. "True to her? When she treats me like that? I took the oath, I did – but what's in it for me?" He licked his paws as he considered his woes. "One last chance," he decided. "I'll give her one last chance. If there's pies at the end of it, it'll all be worth it."

When Tom had made the chocolate cake, he went round the cottage collecting bags and baskets and pieces of rope and packed up the food. Tallulah was very quiet; neither of them could think of anything cheerful to say.

Tom glanced at the clock. "When will you be leaving?"

"About half past ten," Tallulah said. "I want to get all the food set out before the others arrive."

"Will you be all right?" Tom asked, then wished he hadn't. It was the kind of question that Tallulah hated … but she didn't snap at him.

Instead she said, "I wish you were coming with me."

"Me too," Tom told her. "Come on. I'll help you load up."

By the time everything was tied onto the broomstick it was time to go. Sparks jumped on the back, and Tallulah, much to his surprise, kissed Tom goodbye. "Wish me luck."

"I do," Tom said. "I really do." And he stood waving until his sister was out of sight.

Ten minutes later there was another broomstick in the sky. Gertrude Higgins was on her way, Kibble clinging to the back of her broom. Glancing down as she flew past Tabitha Tickle's cottage she cackled happily at the thought of seeing Tallulah humiliated. "Ha!" she crowed. "We'll soon see the end of YOU, Tabitha Tickle!"

Kibble, his stomach rumbling painfully, also saw the cottage. It's now or never, he told himself and, summoning up all his courage, he asked, "Is it today we get the pies?"

"What's that?" Gertrude, interrupted in her self-congratulatory daydream, was irritated.

"I said, do we get the pies today?"

The witch snorted. "Pies? Not for you, Kibble! Not for you! When I'm head witch it'll all be for ME! There'll be nothing for nasty little cats who

steal. Nothing at all—"

"That's it!" Kibble took a deep breath, and jumped. Shutting his eyes, he counted his nine lives as he fell … and landed in the middle of a compost heap. For a moment he lay still, checking he was still in one piece, but then he scrambled to his feet – and saw

Tom coming out of his grandmother's shed.

The boy was looking gloomy, and Kibble wondered if he'd made a terrible mistake.

"Did you mean it?" he asked urgently. "You'll keep me safe?"

Tom, hardly daring to believe his eyes, stared at the cat – then nodded. "I promise."

"Okeydoke. Here's what she wrote: 'a cheese and tomato pizza big enough to feed six hungry witches'!"

"WHAT?" Tom's jaw dropped.

Gargle, who had been watching from a nearby tree, fluffed his feathers in astonishment. "*Awk! Matey mine, what's to do?*"

Tom swung round to look at him. "How can I get to the meeting so I can tell Lou? I still can't wake Grandmother up – I've been trying and trying. Lou HAS to join the Circle!"

"Haven't you got a broomstick?" Kibble asked.

Tom blinked. "A broomstick?"

"You flew one before, didn't you?" the cat pointed out.

"I haven't – oh!" Tom's eye had fallen on the kitchen mop propped against the wall. "I wonder…" He snatched it up. "Come on – let's give it a try!"

Chapter Fifteen

TALLULAH and her laden broomstick arrived safely
in the clearing. She was greeted by Madam Mavis
and Miss Dolly; Miss Dolly hugged her warmly,
and Fluffikins wove in and out of her legs purring
enthusiastically.

"I think I've got everything," Tallulah told them
as she began to unpack Tom's parcels. Madam
Mavis smiled, and snapped her fingers … and a
long table appeared, together with six chairs. Miss
Dolly laughed, and pointed, and the table was
covered with a rose-embroidered cloth laid with
plates and bowls and knives and forks and spoons.

Leonora arrived as the final parcel of food was being opened. She gave Tallulah a chilly nod, and sat down on a chair.

"No crow, Leonora?" Madam Mavis asked.

"Stupid bird escaped." Leonora glanced at Tallulah, but said nothing more. She had realized, too late, that she had furthered Gertrude's chances of becoming head witch, and that thought was very scary indeed.

Dulcie was the next to fly down; she gave a shrill squeak of excitement when she saw the food. "Dear Tallulah, how clever you are! I didn't have any lunch because I was so looking forward to tonight."

Tallulah smiled, although she was feeling anything but confident. What would happen when Gertrude arrived?

She didn't have long to wait; with a swoosh of her broomstick Gertrude Higgins circled the clearing before landing beside the table. Her eyes gleamed when she saw the chocolate birthday cake, and she gave a triumphant sneer. "So, Tallulah Tickle… The time has come to see if you have passed your test!"

"I think we should thank Tallulah before we do anything else," Madam Mavis said. "Whatever the result, she has brought a wonderful cake and a delicious feast."

There was a ripple of applause, which Gertrude ignored. "Bring out the box!" she demanded.

"Why don't we eat first?" Madam Mavis suggested. She had seen Gertrude's sneer and knew Tallulah had failed, but she was hoping to put off the moment of revelation as long as possible.

"No!" Gertrude banged the table with her fist so hard the plates rattled. "I won't share my birthday feast with a failed apprentice!"

Madam Mavis sighed. "Very well, then." She reached into the air and the box appeared in her hand. Slowly she opened it. Gertrude's outburst had made the atmosphere electric; the other witches were silent, all eyes on Madam Mavis. She picked out the first paper. "Tuna casserole."

Miss Dolly clapped her hands. "And it looks delicious!"

"Broomstick apple pie."

Leonora gave Tallulah a sharp look. "Almost perfect."

"Jam roly-poly pudding."

"That's mine." Dulcie gave a nervous giggle. "I'm such a silly billy I wrote down the first thing that came into my head! Tallulah, dear, do tell! How did you make it roll up so neatly?"

"Not now, Dulcie." Gertrude's face was that of a hungry ferret. "Mavis! My paper – if you please!"

Madam Mavis took the last paper from the box. "As you'll all remember," she said, "I told Tallulah what my favorite dish was at our last meeting. I'm sure you'll agree that the macaroni

and cheese on the table is an excellent example; I can hardly wait to try it."

Gertrude Higgins reared up, eyes flashing. "This is ridiculous! Read the paper."

Mavis sighed. "Gather round, ladies."

As the witches surrounded her, Tallulah's heart beat faster – and almost jumped into her throat as a figure came flying into the center of the circle, landing with a crash. "TOM!"

Tom dropped the mop and stood up. "It's pizza! That's what she chose … a cheese and tomato pizza big enough for six hungry witches!"

"That's right!" Tallulah ran to stand beside her brother, her mind whirling. "Cheese and tomato pizza. Too big to carry on a broomstick!"

"NO!" Gertrude's face was a livid purple. "She's a cheat! She's a CHEAT, I tell you! A sneaky little cheat who came creeping to my house to peer through my windows – and I caught her. I caught her with my trick … chocolate cake, I wrote, and what has she made? Exactly that!"

Tom took a step forward. "My sister's not a cheat. She's as brave as brave can be. Yes, we did come to your house, but we came because we absolutely had to. We were desperate! Lou's got to save our grandmother – she's been mad for months, and now she won't wake up…" He stopped; suddenly there was a lump in his throat.

Tallulah took a deep breath. "Tom's right. That's why we came. And we did see the recipe – but that wasn't all we saw. We saw this!" And she pulled a faded purple flower from the bottom of her bag. As she held it out there was a sharp intake of breath from the other witches.

Gertrude's eyes flickered, but she launched straight back into the attack. "So? An Agony flower! What of it? Am I not allowed to grow what I want in my garden?"

"But they're evil!" Tallulah turned to Madam Mavis. "They are, aren't they?"

Madam Mavis nodded. "They're only ever used in Black Magic spells."

"Spells." Tom folded his arms. "Just what I thought."

"Wait, Tom!" Tallulah put a restraining hand on his arm. "Madam Mavis – what flowers do you send my grandmother every month?"

"Roses," the head witch said. "Why do you want to know?"

Miss Dolly, who had been listening intently, nodded. "Roses from my garden…"

"And who delivers them?" Tallulah demanded.

Madam Mavis and Miss Dolly turned to look at Gertrude. She paled under their accusing gaze. "You've no proof! No proof at all. I took her the roses – I did! I did! Someone else must have changed them for the Agonies. It wasn't me – it wasn't me, I tell you!"

The head witch's eyes were steely cold. "Changing them? Who said anything about changing the flowers, Gertrude Higgins?"

Gertrude gave a harsh gasp. "She did! He did!" She pointed at Tallulah and Tom with a long bony finger, but it was no use. Madam Mavis Mortlock had heard enough.

"Gertrude Higgins! You have broken the fundamental rule of the Chumley Charmed Circle. For using Black Magic you are banned, now and forever, and you will never EVER return!"

She waved her hand, and Gertrude, unable to

resist, found herself traveling
backward faster and faster
until she vanished into
the darkness of the
night.

Chapter Sixteen

MADAM MAVIS MORTLOCK rubbed her hands together as if she was getting rid of something unpleasant, then opened the last paper from the box. "Ha!" she said. "'A cheese and tomato pizza, big enough for six hungry witches.' Tallulah Tickle, may I welcome you back? But not as a mere apprentice – as a witch, and a full member of the Chumley Charmed Circle. And perhaps—" she beckoned Tom to come closer. "Perhaps your brother would consider joining us as well? If I'm right, he had quite a lot to do with this feast!"

Tallulah put her arm round her brother's

shoulders. "He did all the cooking." An anxious look crossed her face. "Is that okay? It wasn't cheating?"

Madam Mavis laughed. "Certainly not. But tell me, Tallulah, what's this about your grandmother? Gertrude always told us that she didn't want any visitors."

With a sigh, Tallulah explained what had happened to Tabitha Tickle. "But now I'm part of the Circle, I can ask for help, can't I?"

"Of course," Madam Mavis said. "But I suspect that you and your brother could be quite a powerful team if you worked together. Look at what you've just done: defeated Gertrude Higgins, and made us a wonderful Midnight Feast ... well, except for the pizza. A shame. I'm very fond of pizza."

Tallulah and Tom looked at each other, and Tom grinned. "Come on, Lou! Let's try!"

"Try what?" his sister asked.

"What about a cheese and tomato pizza for six hungry witches?"

There was a loud and enthusiastic squawk from the branch above their heads. "Point your finger, Miss T! You too, me old buddy!"

"Here goes…" Tallulah pointed at an empty space on the table, and Tom did the same. "Do we say anything?" he asked. "Like abracadabra?"

Tallulah didn't answer. She didn't need to. There was an explosion of brightly colored sparks, and a huge pizza appeared in front of them, smelling delightfully of hot cheese and tomato.

"WOW!" Tom stared first at the pizza, and then at his finger. "We did it."

"So we did!" Tallulah's smile spread from ear to ear. "It's even cut into six slices – no. Hang on a minute! There are seven. Why seven?"

"I expect the seventh slice will be for me." The voice came from a figure who had walked into

the clearing unnoticed. She was wrapped in a long gray cloak; Sparks was on one shoulder and Kibble on the other. Both cats were purring loudly and proudly.

"GRANDMOTHER!" Tallulah and Tom ran to hug her. "Grandmother! You're better!"

"Woke up ten minutes ago," Kibble announced. "Pop! Eyes opened, out of bed … asking where you were. I told her, then we grabbed the garden rake and we flew!"

"NOT comfortable at all," Sparks added. "But here we are!"

Tabitha Tickle put one arm round Tallulah and one round Tom. "From what Kibble told me on the way here, it was you two who broke Gertrude's spell. And goodness me! What a truly amazing feast." She gave Tallulah a fond squeeze. "And six months of your cooking, my darling, have left me hungry enough to eat that pizza all by myself!"

Tallulah blushed. "I wasn't very good, was I? But now Tom and I can work the magic together."

"And I'll never need to worry about meals again!" Tabitha threw back her head and laughed so loudly that Gargle all but fell off his branch. "I hate cooking! Now, get busy, and serve up that feast."

As Tallulah began handing round the food, Kibble came to stand beside Tom. He looked up at the boy, and Tom bent down and stroked his head. "Yes, Kibble," he said. "You'll be my cat. And you deserve a prize." He pointed his finger at the ground – but nothing happened.

Gargle, perched on his branch, flapped his wings. "Ask your sister!"

Tom hesitated, then grinned. "Lou! Can you help me? Point your finger."

Tallulah did as she was asked, and three large pies spun through the air and came to land at the cat's feet.

"There," Tom said. "And I'll make sure you never go hungry again."

Kibble didn't answer. He was too busy eating.

Tallulah watched as Tom knelt down beside Kibble to stroke him, then glanced wistfully at Sparks, still on Tabitha's shoulder. The little cat was looking very happy, and Tallulah tried not to sigh.

"*Arrrk!*" Gargle squawked loudly to catch her attention. "Now your Grandma's safe and well, Miss T, she'll be needing her cat. That being the case, you'll be looking for a companion of your own." He put his head to one side. "Might you consider Mr. Gargle?"

Tallulah's eyes shone. "I can't think of anyone better," she said. "Yes, PLEASE!"

Gargle nodded wisely. "It's just like I said. When you've done good, it pops back out to surprise you."

"It certainly does." Madam Mavis had been listening, and she smiled as she waved her hand. "And now, my dears ... let the Chumley Charmed Circle Midnight Feast begin!"

The Adventures of

ALFIE ONION

VIVIAN FRENCH

illustrated by Marta Kissi

ALFIE ONION is setting out on a great adventure. His brother Magnifico is off to make the family's fortune … and Alfie's carrying his luggage! But it turns out Magnifico hates adventures and Alfie has to save the day – with a little help from his loyal dog, a talking horse, two mice and some meddling magpies.

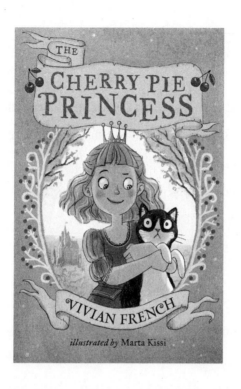

PRINCESS PEONY has a bad feeling that her father might be a tyrant. She doesn't want to believe it, but he has a nasty habit of throwing people in dungeons...

There's a royal party coming up, and the king's in an even worse mood than usual. He flat-out refuses to invite the wicked hag, which can mean only one thing: TROUBLE!

Vivian French

lives in Edinburgh, and writes in a messy workroom stuffed full of fairy tales and folk tales — the stories she loves best. Vivian teaches at Edinburgh College of Art and can be seen at festivals all over the country. She is one of the most borrowed children's authors in UK libraries, and in 2016 was awarded the MBE for services to literature, literacy, illustration and the arts.

Marta Kissi

is an exciting new talent in the world of children's book illustration. Originally from Warsaw, she came to Britain to study Illustration and Animation at Kingston University, and then Art and Design at the Royal College of Art. Her favorite part of being an illustrator is bringing stories to life by creating charming characters and the wonderful worlds they live in. Marta shares a studio in London with her boyfriend and their pet plant Trevor.